NANCY PAULSEN BOOKS

An imprint of Penguin Random House LLC, New York

First published in the United States of America by Nancy Paulsen Books, an imprint of Penguin Random House LLC, 2023

Visit us online at penguinrandomhouse.com.

Library of Congress Cataloging-in-Publication Data

Names: Grady, Ron, author, illustrator.

Title: What does brown mean to you? / Ron Grady.

Description: New York: Nancy Paulsen Books, 2023. | Summary: "A young boy goes about his day, playing, painting, and baking while making positive associations with the color of his brown skin"—Provided by publisher.

Identifiers: LCCN 2022016643 (print) | LCCN 2022016644 (ebook) | ISBN 9780593462881 (hardcover) | ISBN 9780593462904 (kindle edition) | ISBN 9780593462898 (epub)

Subjects: CYAC: Stories in rhyme. | Brown—Fiction. | LCGFT: Stories in rhyme. | Picture books.

Classification: LCC PZ8.3.G7233 Wh 2023 (print) | LCC PZ8.3.G7233 (ebook) | DDC [E]—dc23

LC record available at https://lccn.loc.gov/2022016643

LC ebook record available at https://lccn.loc.gov/2022016644

Manufactured in China

ISBN 9780593462881

1 3 5 7 9 10 8 6 4 2

TOPL

Edited by Stacey Barney
Art direction and design by Marikka Tamura
Text set in Blauth
The art for this book was made first with pencils and finished with pixels.

To Nandi, Manny, and Leni.

Brown is the boy who welcomes the day.

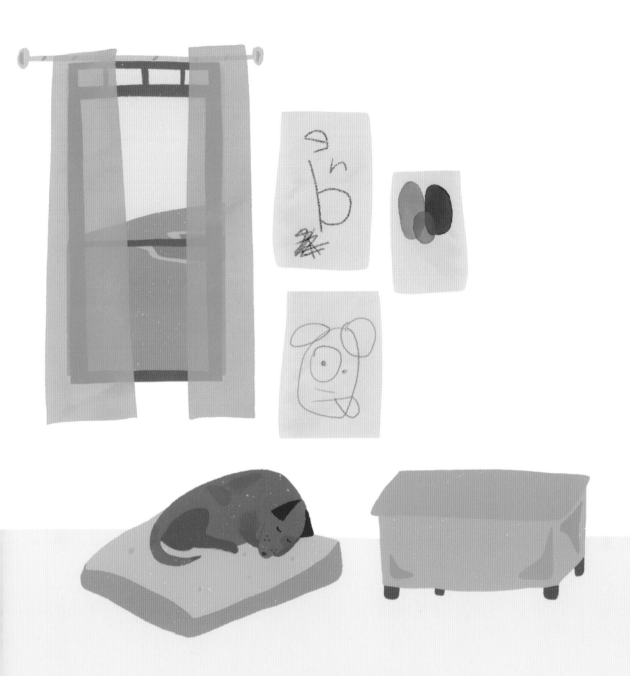

**Brown is the pup
sleeping soundly away.**

Brown is my dad,
who is stirring a mix

for a breakfast of pancakes—my favorite!

Brown are Gram's coffee and
Gramp's morning kiss.

Brown is a lovely moment of bliss.

Brown is the soil that gives life to our plants.

Juicy tomatoes held close in brown hands.

Bess the brown cow is hungry for hay.

Brown are the small eggs the chickens lay.

Brown is sweet syrup drizzled on pancakes so soft.

Brown is the sound of adventure. We're off!

Out from a brown tree into the glorious day,

a brown little bird flies swiftly away.

Brown is the ground where I rest my feet.

Brown is the dirt Percy sniffs

when we hide and we seek.

Slow, careful steps, count them: one, two, and three.

Brown is the best log for balancing!

Next, a quick game of fetch with a bouncy ball.

And then a quick rest on a blanket we sprawl.

Brown is my lookout, from where I can hear
the sound of a storm drawing near.

Brown is
mud,
made by
the rain.

So fun to
jump in
again and
again!

Brown muddy footprints
leading inside

to a brown little boy
who is wiped-off and dry.

Brown is an artist working happily away

on a portrait of family on a gray day.

Brown is a new idea
from an old book.

A book full of recipes to make, bake, and cook.

Brown is a wooden spoon
patiently waiting

for stirring and mixing
before we start baking!

A meal sits before us, our day almost done,
gathered at the table with everyone.

Gramp, Mom, and Benny, Dad and then Gran,
we all give thanks and hold on to brown hands.

Brown is me sharing a new favorite treat,
sweet, gooey goodness so lovely to eat.

Brown is getting down with my mom to James Brown!

Brown is hot cocoa in a mug that is red,
and snuggles at story time right before bed.

A brown fuzzy blanket
I take to my room . . .

where I dream and I wonder:

What does Brown mean to you?